Pippa
and
Poppa

by Anne Cassidy

Illustrated by Philip Norman

W
FRANKLIN WATTS

This edition 2009

Franklin Watts
338 Euston Road
London
NW1 3BH

Franklin Watts Australia
Level 17/207 Kent Street
Sydney
NSW 2000

A CIP catalogue record for this book is available
from the British Library.

ISBN 978 0 7496 9140 0

Series Editor: Louise John
Series Advisor: Dr Barrie Wade
Series Designer: Jason Anscomb

Printed in China

Franklin Watts is a division of
Hachette Children's Books,
an Hachette UK company.
www.hachette.co.uk

For Doll Reynolds
and Pippa – A.C

When Granny went out
for the day, Pippa stayed
with Mum and Ben.

"Look after Pippa,"
Granny said.

"She is very precious."

5

Pippa was sad. She looked
for Granny in the garden ...

in the kitchen ...

and out of the window.

Ben felt sorry for Pippa.

He took her into the
garden to play football.

"Oh, no!" shouted Ben.

"Pippa has escaped."

Mum and Ben looked for
Pippa in the street.

Then they knocked on all
the doors.

"Granny will be very upset," said Mum.

"Pippa is very precious."

"Let's go to the Dog's Home," said Ben.

"Maybe someone will have found Pippa."

At the Dog's Home, Ruby
showed them round.

Ben couldn't see Pippa
anywhere.

"We found this little dog last week," said Ruby.

"His name is Poppa."

"I've got an idea!" said Ben.

Mum, Ben and Ruby had
to get Poppa ready.

Mum and Ben took Poppa
to Granny's house.

Granny looked surprised.

"But Pippa is here!"
said Granny.

"She was waiting for me when I got home."

Now Granny has two dogs,
Pippa **and** Poppa.

They are both very precious.

Puzzle 1

Put these pictures in the correct order.
Now tell the story in your own words.
How short can you make the story?

Puzzle 2

shy   lazy

naughty

upset   tired

worried

surprised   cheerful

confused

Choose the words which best describe
each character. Can you think of any
more? Pretend to be one of the characters!

Answers

Puzzle 1

The correct order is:

1c, 2f, 3d, 4a, 5e, 6b

Puzzle 2

Pippa: naughty, shy

Ben: upset, worried

Granny: confused, surprised

Look out for more Leapfrog stories:

The Little Star
ISBN 978 0 7496 3833 7

Recycled!
ISBN 978 0 7496 4388 1

Jack's Party
ISBN 978 0 7496 4389 8

The Crying Princess
ISBN 978 0 7496 4632 5

Jasper and Jess
ISBN 978 0 7496 4081 1

The Lazy Scarecrow
ISBN 978 0 7496 4082 8

Big Bad Blob
ISBN 978 0 7496 7092 4*
ISBN 978 0 7496 7796 1

Cara's Breakfast
ISBN 978 0 7496 7093 1*
ISBN 978 0 7496 7797 8

Croc's Tooth
ISBN 978 0 7496 7799 2

The Magic Word
ISBN 978 0 7496 7096 2*
ISBN 978 0 7496 7800 5

Tim's Tent
ISBN 978 0 7496 7801 2

Why Not?
ISBN 978 0 7496 7094 8*
ISBN 978 0 7496 7798 5

Sticky Vickie
ISBN 978 0 7496 7986 6

Handyman Doug
ISBN 978 0 7496 7987 3

Billy and the Wizard
ISBN 978 0 7496 7985 9

Sam's Spots
ISBN 978 0 7496 7976 7*
ISBN 978 0 7496 7984 2

Bill's Baggy Trousers
ISBN 978 0 7496 3829 0

Bill's Bouncy Shoes
ISBN 978 0 7496 7990 3

Little Joe's Big Race
ISBN 978 0 7496 3832 0

Little Joe's Balloon Race
ISBN 978 0 7496 7989 7

Felix on the Move
ISBN 978 0 7496 4387 4

Felix and the Kitten
ISBN 978 0 7496 7988 0

The Cheeky Monkey
ISBN 978 0 7496 3830 6

Cheeky Monkey on Holiday
ISBN 978 0 7496 7991 0

For details of all our titles go to: www.franklinwatts.co.uk

*hardback